Seriously Silly Stories

SNOW WHITE
and the
SEVEN ALIENS

Compass Point Books
151 Good Counsel Drive
P. O. Box 669
Mankato, MN 56002-0669

Visit Compass Point Books on the Internet at *www.compasspointbooks.com*
or e-mail your request to *custserv@compasspointbooks.com*

 This book was manufactured with paper containing
at least 10 percent post-consumer waste.

Library of Congress Cataloging-in-Publication Data
Anholt, Laurence.
    Snow White and the Seven Aliens / by Laurence Anholt. Illustrated by Arthur Robins.
        p. cm. — (Seriously silly stories)
Summary: In this version of the classic fairy tale "Snow White," pop stardom is the
sought-after prize, and seven singing aliens are Snow White's back-up singers.
ISBN 978-0-7565-0635-3 (Hardcover)
    [1. Fairy tales. 2. Humorous stories.] I. Title II. Series: Anholt, Laurence. Seriously
silly stories.
    bPZ8.A577 Sn 2004
    [E]—dc22   2003017957

For more information on this topic, use FactHound.

1. Go to *www.facthound.com*
2. Type in this book ID: 0756506352
3. Click on the *Fetch It* button.

FactHound will find the best Web sites for you.

About the Author
Laurence Anholt is one of the UK's leading authors. From his home in Dorset,
he has produced more than 80 books, which are published all around the world.
His Seriously Silly Stories have won numerous awards, including the Smarties
Gold Award for "Snow White and the Seven Aliens."

About the Illustrator
Arthur Robins has illustrated more than 50 picture books, all of them highly
successful and popular titles, and is the illustrator for all the Seriously Silly
Stories. His energetic and fun-filled drawings have been featured in countless
magazines, advertisements, and animations. He lives with his wife and two
daughters in Surrey, England.

First published in Great Britain by Orchard Books, 96 Leonard Street, London EC2A 4XD

Text © Laurence Anholt 1998/Illustrations © Arthur Robins 1998

Seriously Silly Stories

SNOW WHITE
and the
SEVEN ALIENS

Written by Laurence Anholt
Illustrated by Arthur Robins

Compass Point Books ✦ Minneapolis, Minnesota

4

Snow White dreamed of becoming a pop star. She wanted to be number one in the charts, just like her hero, Hank Hunk from Boysbop.

Snow White had a beautiful voice. She was a great dancer, too. And she could even write her own songs.

Only one thing stood in her way—her wicked stepmother.

Once upon a time Snow White's stepmother had been a famous pop star.

She had been the Mean Queen, lead singer in The Wonderful Wicked Witches. But now her voice was croaky, and she was no longer a star. She had become mad with jealousy of Snow White.

"You will never be famous like me!" she would hiss. "You look too… ordinary. You don't even have a band. And besides, your nose is too small."

Then, the Mean Queen would storm out of the room, leaving poor Snow White to weep under the Boysbop posters in her bedroom.

Snow White's father was a kind little man. He liked doing jigsaw puzzles and making small clay models. Although he loved his daughter, he was not strong enough to stand up to his wife.

The Mean Queen had a huge dressing room at the top of the house, with dozens of mirrors and shelves of makeup, as if she were still a great star.

And sometimes she forced her poor husband to sit behind the dressing-table mirror and tell her that she was still beautiful.

Mirror, mirror, on the wall,
Who has the cutest
nose of all?

From behind the mirror, her terrified husband would reply:

Mean Queen, you look
so neat.
With a nose as perfect
as a boiled sweet.

Then, the Mean Queen would scream with laughter and march around the house croaking her ancient songs, and remembering the day when The Wonderful Wicked Witches had appeared on the Christmas edition of "Top of the Pops."

Now, Snow White often sat in the garden surrounded by little birdies and bunny rabbits, singing quietly in her beautiful clear voice. When she looked down, the Mean Queen would almost choke with rage.

Day by day, the Mean Queen could see that Snow White was growing into a very beautiful young woman. With that tiny pink nose… how the Mean Queen hated her.

Only the mirror brought her comfort.

And the mirror would reply:

If you push me, I must admit,
Snow White's nose is a decent fit.
But your nose, oh Queen, is
really small,
In fact, it's hardly there at all.

And so it went on, until one terrible night, Snow White's father could stand the lies no longer. The Mean Queen demanded:

Mirror, mirror above the sink,

Tell me what you REALLY think.

It's time you started coming clean—
CHOOSE SNOW WHITE—

OR ME, YOUR QUEEN.

In a tiny, trembling voice, the mirror replied:

All right. I've really had enough,
I'm fed up with the lies and stuff.
You are past it, old and sad,
Crinkly, wrinkly—really bad.
Your nose is sort of long and hairy,
Beside you, Snow White
is a Christmas fairy!

The Mean Queen leaped to her feet. With a sweep of her bony hand, she sent her makeup and bottles of perfume crashing to the floor. She seized her husband by his collar, and lifted him off his feet.

"Get Snow White OUT OF MY HOUSE," she spat into his terrified face. "Make sure she NEVER EVER returns."

The poor man crawled toward the door. But the Mean Queen had one more order—something so terrible that her husband quaked in his sandals.

25

And so, Snow White's father led his beautiful daughter far into the wild and dangerous city. With tears streaming down his face, he bought her an all-day bus pass and kissed his sweet daughter good-bye.

Of course, he could not bring himself to cut off that precious snubby nose, so he quickly made a false one out of some pink modeling clay, which he always carried in his pocket.

This he brought back to the Mean Queen on a cocktail stick.

When the Mean Queen saw the little nose, she screamed with laughter all over again. Then she did something so ghastly that her husband felt quite ill.

She took the clay nose, dipped it in mayonnaise, and ATE IT, with a side salad and french fries.

"Mmm!!" she said, licking her lips. "Tasty!"

Meanwhile, poor Snow White wandered through the city, lost and alone.

It grew dark, and she started to feel afraid. Then, in the distance, she saw a dim green light between the buildings. Faint with hunger, she stumbled toward it and found herself in a clearing by a parking lot.

There in front of her was... a gleaming silver spacecraft!

A little ladder led up to a door where a flashing neon sign said:

SWINGING SPACESHIP
NIGHTCLUB.

Under this was pinned another smaller notice. This one read:

Cleaner wanted. Apply within.

Too tired to feel afraid, Snow White pushed the doorbell. Quietly, the door slid open, and she stepped nervously inside.

And so it was that Snow White began her new life as a cleaner at the Swinging Spaceship Night Club. The hours were long, the pay was poor, but at least some good bands played from time to time.

"Who knows?" sighed Snow White. "Perhaps I might even hear Hank Hunk from Boysbop one day!"

One evening, Snow White was told to prepare the dressing room for a special band who would be playing that night.

In the dressing room she found seven identical chairs. Laid neatly on the seven identical chairs were seven identical space helmets.

I wonder who will be changing in here? she thought.

Just then, she heard strange voices singing outside in the corridor…

"Hi ho, hi ho, it's off to space we go…"

What an awful song, thought Snow White. I wonder who wrote those terrible lyrics?

The door opened and in stepped seven of the most extraordinary creatures Snow White had ever seen.

"Hi," said the first stranger. "We are the Seven Aliens. We are booked to perform tonight. We are number 4,324 in the pop charts, you know. Meet the band…"

"And what about you?" laughed Snow White, pointing at the very funny-looking alien who had spoken to her first. "What is your name?"

"He's BOTTY!!" shouted all the other aliens together.

"Well," giggled Snow White. "I am very pleased to meet you. Now, if you like, I will polish your space helmets before you go on stage."

While Snow White polished, she sang a sad and beautiful song. The Seven Aliens were entranced.

"That was wonderful," gurgled Grotty when she had finished. "Tell us your name."

"I am Snow White," said Snow White.

"Oh, Snow White," sniffed Snotty. "The truth is, we cannot sing for toffee and the only words we can think of are 'hi ho, hi ho'.

If you would join our band, we would blast up the charts like a rocket into space."

And so it was that Snow White and the Seven Aliens played their very first gig at the Swinging Spaceship Nightclub.

41

Meanwhile, at home, Snow White's father wept over his lost daughter until his jigsaw puzzles were soggy. The Mean Queen, on the other hand, was in a very good mood. She went to admire herself in her magic mirror.

Mirror, mirror, spill the beans,
Am I now the queen of queens?
Now Snow White's nose is in my tummy,
You must admit I look quite yummy.

But to her horror the mirror replied:

Here's the news flash of the day:
that nose was made of modeling clay
Snow White's nose is on her face.
She's with some guys from outer space.

The Mean Queen turned purple. She smashed the mirror into a thousand jagged pieces.

Back at the Swinging Spaceship Nightclub, Snow White and the Seven Aliens had been a huge success. A record producer had heard them play and signed them on the spot.

Snow White's dream was coming true.

As Christmas approached, her single "Snow White Alien Rap" crept higher and higher up the charts, eventually even overtaking Hank Hunk and Boysbop.

Snow White and the Seven Aliens were booked to appear on the Christmas edition of "Top of the Pops."

Snow White was terribly nervous. She was sure the Mean Queen would do something to spoil her good fortune. The aliens made her promise to lock her dressing room door and not let anyone in but them.

But with only half an hour to go before the program, someone rattled the door handle, and a voice called…

Snow White thought the voice sounded a little strange, but she just had to see if it was really Hank Hunk from Boysbop there to see her!

She opened the door a tiny crack.

In burst a tall figure with blonde hair.

It looked like Hank Hunk... But surely there was something strange about his nose?

Ah, ha, hah, haar!!!

Alas! It was the Mean Queen.

When the aliens came to collect Snow White they found her completely frozen with stage fright. No matter how they tried to reassure her, she simply could not move her arms and legs, let alone dance or sing.

In despair, they carried her, like a statue, out of the dressing room and laid her gently on the stage.

"It's no use," bawled Botty. "We'll have to sing 'hi ho, hi ho...'"

The program started.

"FANTABULOUS Christmas Greetings, pop fans," called the announcer. "We've got a SENSATIONAL seasonal line up for you, including the incredible new discovery, Snow White and those Seven EXTREMELY STRANGE Aliens. We've also got Hank Hunk and Boysbop, and later…"

ON AIR

SNOW
WHITE

53

Snow White was still unable to move. To the Seven Aliens, it seemed like a hundred years passed by. Then, at the back of the studio, someone began to push his way through the crowd.

"Let me through," he said. "I'm a qualified heartthrob. I simply must see her."

It was Hank Hunk! This time it really was him. Snow White's heart began to flutter.

"Oh, Snow White," whispered Hank, "please sing. Sing for me." He bent towards Snow White. A long blond curl fell across one eye. Gently, he kissed her lips.

Snow White jumped to her feet.
"OK BOYS. Let's GROOVE!!"
she shouted.

Snow White and the Seven Aliens jumped into the spotlight and began to play. Across the nation, every family threw down their Christmas cookies and began dancing to the fantastic sounds on TV.

Everybody, except one person. High in her dark dressing room, the Mean Queen stared into her shattered mirror and muttered:

Mirror, mirror, smashed to bits,
Today I really feel...the PITS!

But her husband, jiving in front of the TV, called up to her:

That's funny, honey, I feel quite perky,
Come downstairs and have some turkey.
If you're good, you never know,
I might get out the mistletoe.

On New Year's Eve, there were seven special guests at Hank and Snow White's wedding. Their names were Scotty, Spotty, Dotty, Snotty, Potty, Grotty, and Botty.

And they all blasted off for a honeymoon in the stars.

"Hi ho, hi ho…"